# One More Blanket

WRITTEN BY
## Shawn Finger

ILLUSTRATED BY
## Kim Grimm

Oatmeal Bear can be ordered in the REcreationsyarn shop on etsy.com.

ISBN-13:
978-1502340993

ISBN-10:
1502340992

To Ashlynn, Lucas, Jacob, Levi and the dreams they chase.

Tonight as you lie down my dear
to rest your busy head

one blanket

soft and warm and still
I'll place upon your bed.

Tucked gently in from every

I'll get you nice and

One blanket nestled chin

our good-night, all-night

side

snug

to toes

hug.

I'll kiss
your head
so gratefully

then slowly
close your door

knowing I'll be back again
to tuck you in once more.

For after you fall fast asleep
the dreams within your head

will twist and tug and pull and kick
this blanket from your bed.

Are you climbing trees with monkeys?

Or basking in the sun?

Did you hit a **home run**, slugger?

Knocking in the winning run?

So big you dream!

So fast! So high!

You run without a pause,
in your superhero slumber
where there's no rest for your cause.

I'm guessing from the poses
that your sleeping self assumes

that in your dreams you're flying

with good witches on their brooms.

Or do you roam with dinosaurs?

Do you drift through clouds and sky?
And do you dream of me?

The way you wiggle, flop and squirm
a busy sleep, it seems
one blanket just can't keep up
with the power of your dreams.

So back I'll come into your room
with one more cozy spread

replacing what's been kicked off
by the visions in your head.

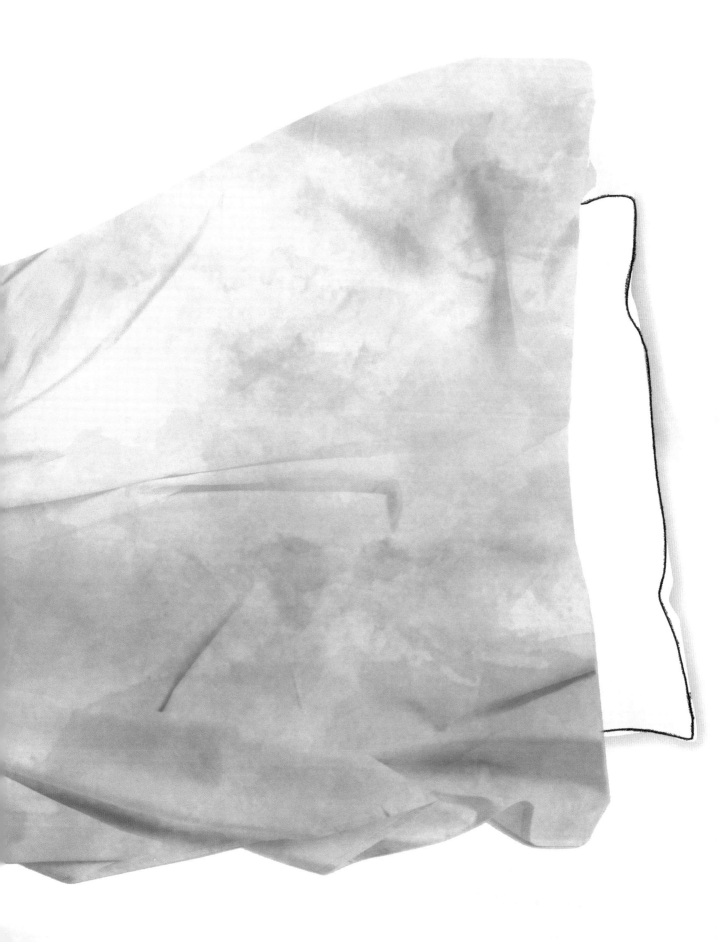

And when you wake tomorrow
as night's sky fades to light

you'll find this warm reminder
of my visit in the night.

One more blanket on your bed
my quiet gift to you

Because however big your dreams may be
I love you more, times two.

## ABOUT THE AUTHORS

Shawn Finger and Kim Grimm are friends.
Kim's names rhyme, which is
awesome-awesome-bo-bawesome.
Shawn's last name makes cashiers giggle
and her first name, wait, her?
They each live in Missouri with their
husbands, kids and dogs, and both very
much enjoy tomato soup and blankets.

**Project ♥ Linus**
*Providing Security Through Blankets*

A portion of the proceeds from each first edition copy of One More Blanket goes to support Project Linus,
an organization providing new, handmade blankets to seriously ill or traumatized children. Learn more at projectlinus.org.

Made in the USA
Lexington, KY
24 January 2015